HOW TO CATCH
A BUTTERFLY

All inquiries should be addressed to:
Barron's Educational Series, Inc.
250 Wireless Boulevard
Hauppauge, NY 11788

International Standard Book Number 0-8120-9246-5

Library of Congress Catalog Card Number 95-21026

Library of Congress Cataloging-in-Publication Data

Foster, Kelli C.
    How to catch a butterfly / by Foster & Erickson ; illustrations by
Kerri Gifford.
        p. cm. — (Get ready—get set—read!)
        Summary: A fox, July, and an otter, Small Fry, first try to catch a
butterfly and when that fails, a firefly.
        ISBN 0-8120-9246-5
        (1. Animals—Fiction. 2. Stories in rhyme.) I. Erickson, Gina Clegg.
II. Gifford, Kerri, ill. III. Title. IV. Series: Erickson, Gina Clegg.
Get ready—get set—read!
PZ8.3.F813Ho   1996
(E)—dc20   95-21026
                                                             CIP
                                                             AC

PRINTED IN HONG KONG
6789 9927   987654

GET READY...GET SET...READ!

HOW TO CATCH A BUTTERFLY

by
Foster & Erickson

Illustrations by
Kerri Gifford

BARRON'S

"Small Fry, let's try
to catch the bugs
as they fly by."

"Why, July?" asked Small Fry.
But July did not reply.

"Look! I spy a butterfly,"
cried July.

"Now, Small Fry,
you must be sly.
Butterflies are very shy."

But trying as hard
as she could try,

she could not catch
that butterfly.

9

"Forget the butterfly,
Small Fry. Let's try
to catch that firefly."

"Why, July?" asked Small Fry.
But July did not reply.

"Oh no!
There goes the firefly.
Let's get that dragonfly!"

12

"Now, Small Fry,
be fast on this try.
Dragonflies are very spry."

But trying as hard
as she could try,

she could not catch
that dragonfly.

"Let's sit and watch the sky,"
said July.

"My, oh my, now I see.
I can't catch them. . .

"... I'll let them catch me!"

The End

The Y Word Family

butterfly
dragonfly
firefly
fly
fry
July
my
reply
shy
sky
sly
spry
spy
trying
why

Sight Words

I'm
I'll
goes
hard
asked
catch
going
watch
forget
pretty

Dear Parents and Educators:

Welcome to *Get Ready...Get Set...Read!*

We've created these books to introduce children to the magic of reading.

Each story in the series is built around one or two word families. For example, *A Mop for Pop* uses the OP word family. Letters and letter blends are added to OP to form words such as TOP, LOP, and STOP. As you can see, once children are able to read OP, it is a simple task for them to read the entire word family. In addition to word families, we have used a limited number of "sight words." These are words found to occur with high frequency in the books your child will soon be reading. Being able to identify sight words greatly increases reading skill.

You might find the steps outlined on the facing page useful in guiding your work with your beginning reader.

We had great fun creating these books, and great pleasure sharing them with our children. We hope *Get Ready...Get Set...Read!* helps make this first step in reading fun for you and your new reader.

Kelli C. Foster, PhD
Educational Psychologist

Gina Clegg Erickson, MA
Reading Specialist

Guidelines for Using *Get Ready...Get Set...Read!*

Step 1.   Read the story to your child.

Step 2.   Have your child read the Word Family list
             aloud several times.

Step 3.   Invent new words for the list. Print each new
             combination for your child to read.
             Remember, nonsense words can be used
             (*dat, kat, gat*).

Step 4.   Read the story *with* your child. He or she reads
             all of the Word Family words; you read the rest.

Step 5.   Have your child read the Sight Word list
             aloud several times.

Step 6.   Read the story *with* your child again. This time
             he or she reads the words from both lists;
             you read the rest.

Step 7.   Your child reads the entire book to you!

There are five sets of books in the

Series. Each set consists of five **FIRST BOOKS**
and two **BRING-IT-ALL-TOGETHER BOOKS**.

SET 1

is the first set your children should read.
The word families are selected from the short vowel sounds:
at, **ed**, **ish** and **im**, **op**, **ug**.

SET 2

provides more practice
with short vowel sounds:
an and **and**, **et**, **ip**, **og**, **ub**.

SET 3

focuses on
long vowel sounds:
ake, **eep**, **ide** and **ine**, **oke** and **ose**, **ue** and **ute**.

SET 4

introduces the idea that the word family sounds
can be spelled two different ways:
ale/ail, een/ean, ight/ite, ote/oat, oon/une.

SET 5

acquaints children with word families that
do not follow the rules for long and short vowel sounds:
all, **ound**, **y**, **ow**, **ew**.